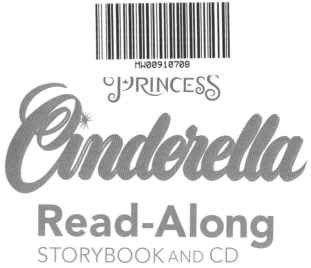

PRINCESS
Cinderella
Read-Along
STORYBOOK AND CD

This is the story of *Cinderella*. You can read along with me in your book. You will know it is time to turn the page when you hear the Fairy Godmother wave her magic wand like this. . . . Let's begin now.

Play Track 1 on your CD now!

Printed in the United States of America

First Edition, July 2018   10 9 8 7 6 5 4 3 2

Library of Congress Control Number: 2018935343

ISBN 978-1-368-02809-7   FAC-038091-20051

For more Disney Press fun, visit www.disneybooks.com

 **DISNEY PRESS**

Los Angeles • New York

SUSTAINABLE FORESTRY INITIATIVE — Certified Sourcing
www.sfiprogram.org
SFI-00993
Logo Applies to Text Stock Only

Once there was a kind and beautiful girl named Cinderella,
who lived with her cruel stepmother and two selfish stepsisters,
Anastasia and Drizella.

Every morning, Cinderella told her little mice and bird friends about her dreams. "They're wishes my heart makes when I'm asleep. If I believe in them, someday they'll come true!"

Then one day an announcement arrived from the palace. "The King is giving a royal ball in honor of the Prince. Every maiden in the kingdom is commanded to come!"

The stepsisters were thrilled, and so was Cinderella. "Every maiden! That means I can go, too!"

Her stepsisters laughed, but her stepmother smiled slyly. "You may go, Cinderella, if you do all your work. And if you find something suitable to wear!"

All that day, Cinderella's stepmother and stepsisters shouted orders at her. Cinderella's mice and bird friends watched sadly.

"Poor Cinderelly."

"They keeping her so busy she never get her dress done."

Then they had an idea! "We can do it!" Soon they were happily snipping and stitching to make a lovely dress for Cinderella.

When evening came, tired Cinderella trudged up the stairs to her tiny attic room.

When she saw the pretty gown they had made for her, Cinderella could hardly speak. "Oh! How can I ever . . . oh, thank you so much!"

Dressed and ready, Cinderella ran downstairs. "Wait! Please! Wait for me!"

Anastasia and Drizella saw how lovely Cinderella looked and flew into a jealous rage. They ripped her dress to shreds.

"That's enough, girls," Lady Tremaine said at last. "Don't upset yourselves before the ball. It's time to go."

Laughing cruelly, they left.

Cinderella was heartbroken. She ran into the garden, weeping. "It's no use. There's nothing left to believe in!"

Suddenly, she heard a cheery voice. "Nonsense, child. If you didn't believe, I wouldn't be here . . . and here I am!"

Cinderella looked up and saw an older woman smiling at her. "I'm your fairy godmother. Dry your tears. We must hurry!"

"First we need a pumpkin and some mice. Now for the magic words: bibbidi-bobbidi-boo!" With a wave of her wand, the Fairy Godmother turned the pumpkin into a coach and the mice into white horses.

The Fairy Godmother hurried Cinderella to her coach. "But . . . but . . . my dress."

"Yes, yes . . . it's lovely—
good heavens, child! You can't
go in that. You need a dress.
Well, just leave it to me. What
a gown this will be! Bibbidi-
bobbidi-boo!"

The Fairy Godmother waved her wand, and
Cinderella's rags changed into a shimmering gown. On
her feet, two dainty glass slippers twinkled like stars.
"Oh, it's like a wonderful dream come true!"

But the Fairy Godmother gave Cinderella a warning. "On the stroke of twelve, the spell will be broken and everything will be as it was before."

Cinderella blew the Fairy Godmother a kiss, and the coach sped away toward the castle.

Meanwhile, at the ball, the Grand Duke and the King watched the Prince greet one maiden after another with a polite but bored expression.

Then, suddenly, a hush fell over the ballroom.

The Prince looked toward the grand entrance. A lovely girl in a dress the color of moonlight stood there with all eyes on her. It was Cinderella, but her stepmother and stepsisters didn't recognize her. "Who is she, Mother?"

"I don't know, but she seems familiar."

Prince Charming knew he'd found the girl of his dreams. "May I have this dance?" As the music played, they waltzed around the ballroom and out into the garden. Soon enough, the castle clock began to chime.

"Oh, my goodness! It's midnight! I must go! Good-bye!"

As Cinderella ran away, the Prince rushed after her. "Wait! Come back! I don't even know your name!"

Cinderella darted through the ballroom and raced down the palace steps, losing a glass slipper on the way. The clock chimed on.

Cinderella jumped into her coach and sped away.
Suddenly, the spell was broken. The coach became a
pumpkin, the horses turned back into mice, and Cinderella
was again dressed in rags.

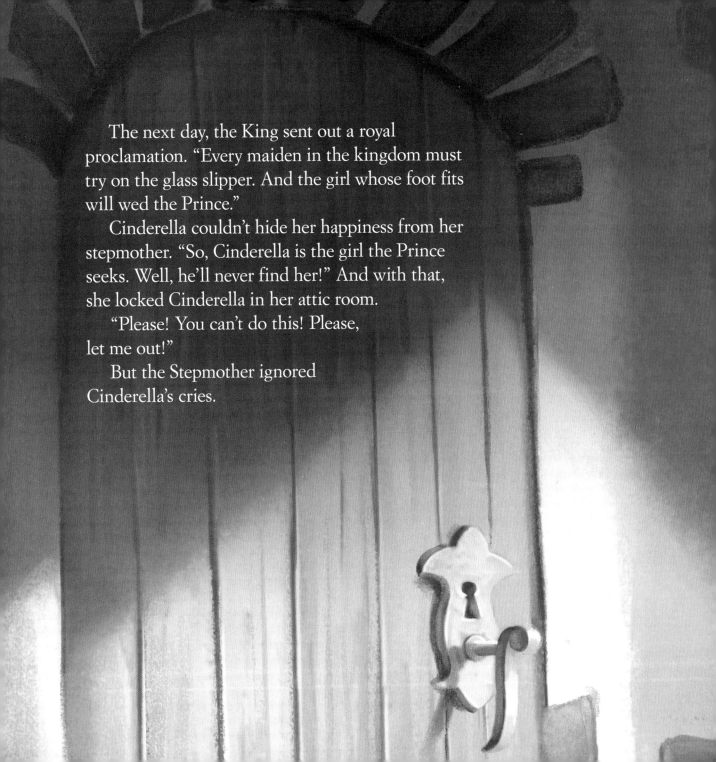

The next day, the King sent out a royal
proclamation. "Every maiden in the kingdom must
try on the glass slipper. And the girl whose foot fits
will wed the Prince."

Cinderella couldn't hide her happiness from her
stepmother. "So, Cinderella is the girl the Prince
seeks. Well, he'll never find her!" And with that,
she locked Cinderella in her attic room.

"Please! You can't do this! Please,
let me out!"

But the Stepmother ignored
Cinderella's cries.

Before long, the Grand Duke and a royal footman arrived with the glass slipper. The Stepmother and stepsisters smiled their sweetest smiles and ushered them in. Both Anastasia and Drizella were eager to find some way to get their feet to fit the slipper!

But though they pushed and shoved, neither of the stepsisters could squeeze a foot into it. "I don't understand why! It always fit perfectly before!"

Meanwhile, Cinderella's mice friends struggled to get the key out of the Stepmother's pocket without her noticing. Then they had to lug it all the way upstairs to the attic. "Thissa way. Up, up, up wif it. Gotta hurry!" They slid it beneath Cinderella's door. She was free!

Downstairs, the Grand Duke knew neither
stepsister was the girl he sought. "Are there any
other maidens in the household?"

"There is no one else, Your Grace."

Just as he turned to leave, Cinderella
ran downstairs.

"Your Grace! Your Grace!
May I try it on?"

As the footman carried the slipper to Cinderella, the Stepmother tripped him, and he fell! The slipper smashed into a hundred pieces. The Grand Duke was horrified!

Cinderella smiled and reached into her pocket. "Perhaps I can help. You see, I have the other slipper."

The Stepmother and stepsisters gasped. With a low bow, the Grand Duke slipped it onto Cinderella's dainty foot. It fit perfectly!

Soon wedding bells rang throughout the kingdom. As the happily married couple rode away in the royal coach, Cinderella realized she had been right, after all. If you keep on believing, your dreams will come true.

And so they all lived happily ever after.

Disney PRINCESS

Beauty and the Beast

Read-Along
STORYBOOK AND CD

Play
Track 2
on your
CD now!

This is the story of *Beauty and the Beast*. You can read
along with me in your book. You will know it is time to
turn the page when you hear the chimes ring like this. . . .
Let's begin now.

DISNEY PRESS
Los Angeles • New York

Once upon a time, a young prince lived in a giant castle. One cold night, an old beggar arrived and offered him a rose in return for shelter. He sneered at her gift and turned her away.

Suddenly, she transformed into a beautiful enchantress. Then she turned the Prince into a hideous beast!

The Enchantress also changed the castle servants into enchanted objects. Then she left behind a magic mirror and the rose. For the spell to be broken, the Prince would have to fall in love, and earn that person's love in return, before the last petal fell.

In a small village nearby lived a beautiful young woman named Belle. As she entered the town bookstore, the owner gave her a book as a gift.

"It's my favorite! Far-off places, daring sword fights, magic spells, a prince in disguise . . . Oh, thank you very much!" Belle rushed outside, reading as she walked.

Soon a hunter named Gaston walked up to her. He grabbed the book from her hands. "It's about time you got your nose out of those books and paid attention to more important things—like me."

Then Gaston's friend LeFou approached. He began to insult Belle's father, Maurice, who was an inventor.

"My father's not crazy! He's a genius!" Then Belle ran toward her father's cottage.

When Belle got home, she told her father that the townspeople were making fun of him.

"Don't worry, Belle. My invention's going to change everything for us." Maurice was hoping to sell his latest creation at the town fair. He hopped on his horse, Philippe, and headed into town.

But Maurice got lost, and he and Philippe ended up in a dark, misty forest. All of a sudden, a pack of wolves surrounded them! Philippe reared and ran away.

Terrified, Maurice raced through the forest, with the wolves right behind him. When he reached a tall gate, he opened it and dashed inside. Then he slammed it shut on the angry wolves.

Belle's father looked up and saw a huge castle. He walked up to the front door and knocked.

"Hello? I've lost my horse, and I need a place to stay for the night."

"Of course, monsieur! You are welcome here!"

Maurice looked down to see a clock and a candelabrum staring up at him. "This is impossible! Why . . . you're alive!"

The candelabrum, named Lumiere, led him inside.

All of a sudden, a loud voice boomed. "There's a stranger here!"
In the shadows lurked a large, hulking figure. It was the Beast!
Maurice pleaded with him. "Please . . . I needed a place to stay."
But the Beast ignored him and dragged him away.

At home, Belle heard a knock on the door.

"Gaston!"

"Belle, there's not a girl in town who wouldn't love to be in your shoes. Do you know why? Because I want to marry you!"

Belle turned his proposal down. She did not like the conceited bully. Disappointed, Gaston left.

A little while later, Belle went outside and found Philippe all alone. "Philippe! What are you doing here? Where's Papa?"

The horse whinnied anxiously. Frightened, Belle quickly leaped onto Philippe, who led her to the mysterious forest. Soon they spotted a castle in the distance.

Belle ran toward the castle and snuck inside. She wandered down a dark, deserted hallway. A few moments later, she found her father locked in a tower. "Papa! We have to get you out of there!"

Suddenly, she heard a loud voice call out from the dark shadows. "What are you doing here?"

Belle gasped. Standing in front of her was a giant beast! "Please, let my father go. Take me instead!"

"You would . . . take his place?"

When Belle promised to stay with the Beast forever, he released Maurice.

Back in the village, Maurice ran into a tavern. There he spotted Gaston and his friends.

"Please, I need your help! A horrible beast has Belle locked in a dungeon!"

The crowd laughed, convinced that he was crazy. But Maurice's wild story gave Gaston an idea. . . .

Inside the castle, the Beast showed Belle to her room. "You can go anywhere you like, except the West Wing."

"What's in the West Wing?"

"It's forbidden!" The Beast stomped off.

Belle ran into her bedroom. "I'll never escape from this prison—*or* see my father again!"

Her new friends—the enchanted household objects—tried to cheer her up, but Belle was too upset.

Later that night, Belle was feeling a little better.
Lumiere led her into the dining room.
    The napkins, dishes, and spoons danced as the
serving pieces carried in tasty food. Belle was delighted!

After dinner, Belle wandered into the forbidden West Wing. There she found the enchanted rose, shimmering beneath a glass dome. She reached out to lift the cover.

But the Beast had been secretly watching her! He was very angry. "I warned you never to come here! Get out!"

Terrified, Belle fled the castle.

Outside, Belle found
Philippe. They galloped
toward the village. All of a
sudden, a pack of hungry
wolves circled them! They
crept toward Belle, baring
their large white fangs.

Just then, the Beast appeared! The wolves began to attack him. With a loud roar, the Beast fought off the wolves. As they ran away, the Beast collapsed in pain. Belle knew this was her chance to escape, but she could not leave him.

"Here, lean against Philippe. I'll help you back to the castle."

When they returned, Belle tended to the Beast's wounds and thanked him for saving her life.

The Beast smiled. To show how grateful he was, he gave her access to the beautiful castle library.

Meanwhile, Gaston was plotting to put Belle's father in an insane asylum. The only way he wouldn't do it was if Belle agreed to marry him. Gaston was convinced that soon she would become his wife.

As more time passed, Belle and the Beast became good friends. One day, she watched as he tried to feed some tiny birds. She realized that he was kind and gentle, despite his gruff appearance.

One night, Belle and the Beast dressed up for a fancy dinner. The Beast even remembered his table manners. They both had a wonderful time.

After dinner, Belle taught the Beast how to dance. They glided gracefully across the floor. The Beast had never been happier.

He asked Belle if she, too, was happy.

"Yes, I only wish I could see my father. I miss him so much."

"There is a way."

Moments later, the Beast brought Belle the magic mirror. When she wished to see her father, Maurice appeared in the glass. He was lost in the woods.

The Beast saw the unhappy look on Belle's face. He decided to let her go—even if it meant he would never be human again. He handed Belle the mirror. "Take it with you, so you'll always have a way to look back and remember me."

Soon Belle found her father. But moments later, a group of men grabbed Maurice to take him away!

Gaston put his arm around Belle. "I can clear up this little misunderstanding—*if* you marry me."

"I'll never marry you. My father's not crazy! I can prove it!" She showed Gaston the magic mirror. An image of the Beast appeared in it.

Gaston shouted, "I say we kill the Beast!" Then he and the villagers headed toward the castle.

When the townsfolk arrived, Gaston forced the Beast onto the roof. As they fought, Gaston lost his balance and fell to the ground.

The Beast suddenly collapsed. Belle ran toward him. She cried, "No! Please! I love you!"

Seconds later, the Beast sprung into the air. He was surrounded by a shimmering glow. Belle had told the Beast that she loved him, which meant that the evil spell that had been cast on him—and all of the household staff—was broken!

The Beast transformed back into a handsome prince!

"Belle, it's me!"

"It *is* you!"

True love had broken the spell, and Belle and the Beast lived happily ever after.

DISNEY PRINCESS

THE LITTLE MERMAID

Read-Along

STORYBOOK AND CD

Play **Track 3** on your CD now!

This is the story of *The Little Mermaid*. You can read along with me in your book. You will know it is time to turn the page when you hear the chimes ring like this. . . . Let's begin now.

DISNEP PRESS

Los Angeles • New York

Once upon a time, a little mermaid named Ariel frolicked below the ocean. She loved to explore sunken ships and look for lost objects. She called to her friend Flounder, a yellow fish. "Come on, Flounder! I'm sure this old boat has lots of human treasure aboard."

"I'm not g-g-going in there! It's spooky!"

"Don't be such a guppy! Follow me!"

When Ariel swam inside the ship's cabin, she discovered a fork. "Oh, my gosh! Have you ever seen anything so wonderful?"

Ariel swam to the water's surface and found her seagull friend. "Scuttle, do you know what this is?" She handed him the fork.

"Judging from my expert knowledge of humans, it's obviously a . . . a . . . *dinglehopper*! Humans use these to straighten their hair."

"Thanks, Scuttle! It's perfect for my collection." And with that, Ariel dove excitedly back underwater.

Soon Ariel arrived in an undersea grotto where she kept her treasures from the human world. She hid her collection there because her father, King Triton, forbade merpeople from having any contact with humans.

That night, Ariel saw strange lights shimmering over the ocean. She and Flounder swam up to investigate.

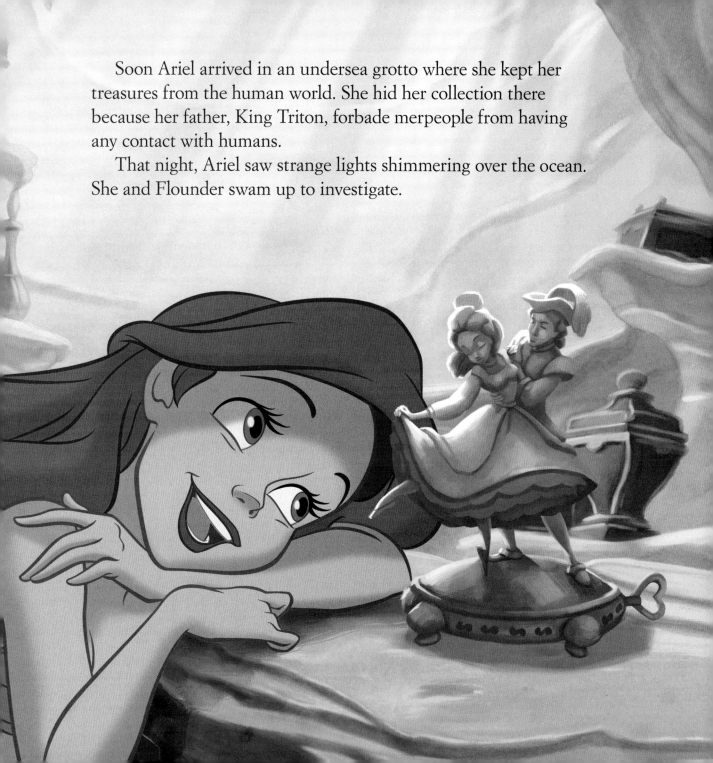

At the surface, they found Scuttle flying over a large sailing ship. "Some celebration, huh, sweetie? It's the birthday of the human they call Prince Eric."

Forgetting her father's rule, Ariel peered in amazement at the young man on the deck. "I've never seen a human this close. He's very handsome."

She watched as Eric's adviser, Grimsby, presented the prince with a birthday gift.

Meanwhile, far beneath the ocean, the wicked sea witch, Ursula, used her magic to spy on Ariel. Ursula was bitter because King Triton had banished her from his kingdom for her evildoing.

"My, my . . . the daughter of the great sea king, Triton, in love with a human! This headstrong, lovesick girl may be the key to my revenge on Triton."

On the surface, a sudden storm whipped across the ocean. The prince took charge. "Stand fast! Secure the rigging!"

Without warning, a huge bolt of lightning struck the vessel. Ariel watched in horror. "Eric's been knocked into the water! I've got to save him!"

With the raging storm swirling around her, Ariel desperately searched for Eric. "Where is he? If I don't find him soon . . . Wait, there he is!"

She took hold of Eric and, using all her strength, managed to pull him to the surface.

As the storm calmed down, Ariel dragged the unconscious prince to shore. "He's still breathing. He must be alive."

Just then, a crab named Sebastian scuttled across the sand. He was the sea king's music director and adviser. "Ariel, get away from that human! Your father forbids contact with them, remember?"

"But Sebastian, why can't I be part of his world?" And she sang about longing to be with Prince Eric forever.

Back in the king's palace, Triton
noticed Ariel floating about as if in
a dream. Suspicious of his daughter's
behavior, Triton summoned Sebastian.
The crab told him the truth about the
shipwreck and the prince.

"Ariel is in love with a *human*?"

King Triton went straight to Ariel's grotto. "How many times have I told you to stay away from those fish-eating barbarians? Humans are dangerous!"

"But, Daddy, I love Eric!"

King Triton would not listen.

Raising his trident, the sea king destroyed all of Ariel's human treasures.
Then he stormed off, leaving the little mermaid in tears.

As she wept,
two eels slithered up
to Ariel and startled her. "Don't be
scared. . . . We represent someone who
can help you!"

They told her they had been sent by
Ursula, who could use her powers to solve
Ariel's troubles.

Ariel was so upset that she followed the eels to Ursula's den. The sea witch offered Ariel a deal. "I'll grant you three days as a human to win your prince. Before sunset on the third day, you must get him to kiss you. If you do, he's yours forever. But if you don't—you'll be mine!"

Ariel took a deep breath and nodded. The sea witch smiled deviously. "Oh, yes, I almost forgot. We haven't discussed payment. I'm not asking much. All I want is—your voice!"

Ariel agreed, and Ursula completed the spell. The evil witch captured Ariel's voice in a seashell locket and turned the mermaid into a human.

With the help of Sebastian and Flounder, Ariel used her new legs to swim awkwardly to shore. She wrapped herself in an old sail. Then she saw Prince Eric walking toward her with his dog, Max. "Down, Max, down! I'm awfully sorry, miss."

Ariel opened her mouth to answer, forgetting that her voice was gone. Eric helped her to her feet.

"Well, the least I can do is make amends for my dog's bad manners. Come on. I'll take you to the palace and get you cleaned up."

The following afternoon, Eric took Ariel for a rowboat ride across a lagoon. Sebastian knew that Ariel only had one more day to get the prince to kiss her, or she would become Ursula's prisoner forever. So he began conducting a sea-creature chorus to set the mood. "C'mon and kiss the girl. . . . The music's working!"

As the prince bent toward her, the boat suddenly tipped, and both Ariel and Eric fell into the water!

From her ocean lair, Ursula saw them tumble into the lagoon. "That was too close for comfort! I can't let Ariel get away that easily!"

She began concocting a magic potion that would transform her into a human. "Soon Triton's daughter will be mine!"

The next morning, Scuttle flew into Ariel's room. The prince had announced his wedding! Ariel's heart skipped a beat at the thought that she had won Eric's love. But when she hurried downstairs, she saw him introducing Grimsby to a mysterious dark-haired maiden.

"Vanessa saved my life. We're going to be married on board ship at sunset."

Ariel was heartbroken. Who was this girl that Eric had suddenly fallen in love with?

A little while later, Ariel and her friends were watching the wedding ship leave the harbor.

Suddenly, Scuttle crash-landed beside them. "When I flew over the boat, I saw Vanessa's reflection in a mirror. She's the sea witch in disguise!"

Flounder helped Ariel swim out to the ship as fast as possible. They arrived just before sunset! Before Vanessa could say *I do*, Scuttle and an army of his friends attacked her.

In the scuffle, the maiden's seashell
necklace crashed to the deck, freeing
Ariel's voice.

Ariel smiled at the prince. "Oh, Eric, I wanted to
tell you—"

Ursula grinned. "You're too late! The sun has set!"

As Ariel felt her body changing back into a mermaid, Ursula pulled her into the water. King Triton confronted the sea witch and made a deal with her to take his daughter's place as Ursula's slave. Instantly, he lost his powers and turned into a helpless sea creature. Ursula became queen of the ocean!

Just then, Prince Eric threw a harpoon at the sea witch to try to stop her. But it simply grazed her arm. Ursula snatched up the king's powerful trident. "You little fool!"

All of a sudden, Ursula turned into an enormous monster and stirred the waters into a deadly whirlpool.

Several old sunken ships rose to the surface. The prince struggled aboard one of them and plunged the sharp prow through the sea witch, destroying her. The mighty force sent Eric flying into the ocean, but he managed to swim to shore before collapsing in exhaustion. King Triton was transformed back into a merman and regained his powers.

Moments later, as the unconscious prince lay on the beach, Ariel perched on a rock and gazed at him. King Triton and Sebastian watched from afar. "She really does love him, doesn't she, Sebastian?"

The sea king wanted his daughter to be happy. So he waved his trident, and Ariel was once again human.

The next day, she and Prince Eric were married aboard a wedding ship. As they kissed, the humans and merpeople sent up a joyful cheer. Ariel and Eric sailed off into the sunset, knowing that they would live happily ever after.